Love Known-Unknown

A Compilation of Timeless Short Stories

AF575057

Joy Mukherji

ISBN 978-93-5559-200-2
© Joy Mukherji 2021
Published in India 2021 by Pencil

A brand of
One Point Six Technologies Pvt. Ltd.
123, Building J2, Shram Seva Premises,
Wadala Truck Terminal, Wadala (E)
Mumbai 400037, Maharashtra, INDIA
E connect@thepencilapp.com
W www.thepencilapp.com

All rights reserved worldwide

No part of this publication may be reproduced, stored in or introduced into a retrieval system, or transmitted, in any form, or by any means (electronic, mechanical, photocopying, recording or otherwise), without the prior written permission of the Publisher. Any person who commits an unauthorized act in relation to this publication can be liable to criminal prosecution and civil claims for damages.

DISCLAIMER: *This is a work of fiction. Names, characters, places, events and incidents are the products of the author's imagination. The opinions expressed in this book do not seek to reflect the views of the Publisher.*

Author biography

Joy Mukherji was born to a Bengali family where creativity and culture flow unhindered. Surrounded by poets, musicians, and filmmakers, writing came naturally to him.

Being an MBA, Joy has worked as a marketer for various advertising agencies and brands for over 12 years. Marketing developed his inquisitiveness towards human psychology and a keen observation led to his journey of penning them down. While cooking up stories is his favourite activity, he also loves to act and is an active theatre enthusiast.

Joy lives in Mumbai with his wife and his daughter, Pearl.

Love Known-Unknown is his debut work.

CONTENTS

UNTIL WE MEET AGAIN 7

WHAT'S IN A NAME 9

BUT TODAY IT RAINED 12

DANCE THE NIGHT AWAY 16

IT WAS YOU 20

MAY GOD GRANT ALL YOUR WISHES 24

THE CARELESS MAN 28

BEAUTY LIES IN THE EYES OF THE BEHOLDER 32

DO NOT CROSS THE LINE 37

LIFE IMPRISONMENT SENTENCE 41

MOM REMEMBERS EVERYTHING 45

Notes 50

Acknowledgements

Growing up, I felt like a compulsive liar. Lying was my only way to escape from reality. Now I know, I wasn't lying, I was simply telling a story. Thank you Maa for bearing with my endless storytelling and letting me be. Also, I wouldn't be writing if it wasn't for your belief that I had an author in me.

Thank you, Babai for making me mentally strong. We may not see eye-to-eye most of the time and despite our differences in how we look at life, thank you for everything. I wouldn't be half of who I am today if it wasn't for your efforts and sacrifices.

Didi and Amlan Da, thank you for your constant presence and guidance in good and bad times. Without you guys, my life would be distraught. You guys are like a persistent blanket over my existence that saves me from all incoming adversaries.

A special thanks to Sweta Samota, the renowned author, for her guidance. The journey would have been a lot difficult without your presence. The learning was truly amazing.

Finally, Neerzari. Thank you would be demeaning for the faith and belief that you have shown in me over the years. You have always been my support, even when the going got tough. Thank you for adjusting to my mood swings, creative loops, lack of time; in general, for being me. Also, for reading the same piece after every edit and still coming up with suggestions, I will always be indebted.

Also, a zillion thanks to every soul who took the time out to read my work and shared their constant feedback. It has not just helped me grow as a writer but changed my general attitude towards life.

UNTIL WE MEET AGAIN

……..Aaooooo (yawn)

I turned over and saw the best thing of my life. Those hands…..they were divine, unlike what I had ever seen. Was I dreaming or is it for real? Pinch, pinch, piiiinch….aooooo…..ok that's real!!!

Hey beautiful. My name is ……. ummm… my name is ….. Ok, now that's some serious performance pressure. Anyway, you can address me by whatever feels good to you because, for eyes like that, I could be anyone. But why ain't you looking at me? And where are you looking really? Well, I am not boasting but one look and you would know that I wasn't blabbering for nothing. Alright, now that's too much of attitude. Honestly, I don't approve so much of priceyness, but I can always make an exception for you. These eyes, those soft hands, those indulgent fingers, that gorgeous lush of hair on your head. They definitely give you an edge over others.

Yet, lady, it's only been me talking all this while. Come on, now. I understand that you don't want to talk straight up but at least, look at me. Trust me, one eye contact would be enough for me to bowl you over. Well, after all, it feels like it's you for whom I exist. Baby, we are meant to be together, forever. I know it. Trust me on this.

Now now, why the hell would you turn the other way? Come on! We do not have the whole day. It's now or never. You got to fall for me before your folks come over, which seems to be soon. God, what is the point of this charm that am oozing if it's not meant for you. Oh God, here they come. Hope you remember me, princess. Yours truly, your first Prince Charming.

(The parents of the baby girl approach her at the hospital nursery and take her away.)

Bye-bye, love……. Until we meet again!!!

Be happy for this moment. This moment is your life.

- Omar Khayyam

WHAT'S IN A NAME

Guru Saakshat Param Bramha,

Tasmai Shree Guruve Namah......

This day was supposed to be like any other day at school. Starting with the morning prayer, a few lectures, a finishing bell, and home. But.... what I see from here today feels like the beginning of something far more dramatic, far more intense. This feeling is not something that I am aware of. Is this what the seniors call, 'Love at first sight?'

By the way, I am a student of 6th standard and am attending the morning assembly. This is where I can see that gorgeous girl in the girls' line. She happens to be in the same standard as me, a different division. But, how on earth have I not seen her before! And what is it about her that I can't take my eyes off!!! This has never happened with the other girls at school. In fact, I don't even like them much.

Anyway, I asked around a little and found out that her father is a senior government official who recently got transferred to our city. Hence, she landed up at my school in the middle of the term. Oh, and her name is…. nope nope nope!!! Not that people wouldn't tell me, or I couldn't find out, it was my whim to hear her name from her mouth and no one else's. Think, I was falling for her if this is what it's supposed to mean. In all these years, this was the most I looked forward to school. At school, I waited for the assembly and then the recess. Finally, my day ended with a glimpse of her before heading home. Even at home, I wasn't feeling myself. All I could think of was her face, her smile, and her dimples. I literally had butterflies in my stomach.

Time flew and after a few eye contacts and random passing smiles, the day came that I had been waiting for. Not that it was planned. But when the time came, I knew that it was my moment to shine. Now there's a thing with us kids, we love to laugh at others' misery. But not this time for me. There she was lying on the playground, crying, and hurt, surrounded by other girls. Immediately, I sprang into action. Approached her with my water bottle, pulled her up on her two feet, and cleaned her knee wound with my own hands. Pure bliss! "By the way, my name is Karan, and yours?", I asked. "Thank you, it's Neha." This is all she said and went away. However, for me, those were Godly words. My first love, Neha. All I could think of was about her, 24x7. Still, could not dare to talk to her ever again.

A few weeks later, Amrit, my buddy at school informed me that her father got transferred yet again and she left. No one knew where and when. That's it, leaving me with just one word to dwell upon, Neha.

A few years later, my English professor who was teaching Shakespeare in the class, excitedly asked, "So class, what's in a name?" All I could utter was, "Neha".

First love is only a little foolishness and a lot of curiosity.

- George Bernard Shaw

BUT TODAY IT RAINED

Rains…. it is less of a word or an event but more of a sentiment. Rainfall brings out different emotions in people. Some are ecstatic when it rains whereas, others are terrified. Hate, anger, frustration, love, peace, rejuvenation. Name an emotion and you will find a taker when it's to do with rains. Talking of rains, it is the most beautiful season to spend in Mumbai. But incessant rainfall often leads to dreadful scenes in the suburbs too. This is my story of one such night.

Hi… my name is Balram. I am a techie who works in an IT firm in Mumbai. However, have not been able to scale up to a client-facing position. Thanks to my poor command over the English language. What to do? My upbringing was in Bihar! Never knew then that English was so important to grow in life. Anyway, what it has also done over time is kill my self-confidence. Not that anybody demeans me. But I tend to get over-conscious when am around people, especially women.

It was late at night, I guess close to 1 am, when I left the office after finishing a demo for the client. August often witnesses extreme rainfall in Mumbai, sometimes even leading to waterlogging. Thankfully, I did not have to chase the rickshawalas as I had my bike. So, I wore my raincoat and helmet and rode towards my home avoiding the obvious potholes on the streets. I must have been a mile away from home when I saw a girl at a passing bus stop, frantically trying to stop a rickshaw. It was pouring at the moment. I thanked my circumstances imagining the hot Maggi I would be devouring on reaching home. I have always been a rain lover and this season, automatically, brought out the romantic in me. Within minutes, I had turned my bike and was now heading towards the girl at the bus stop. Something that I would never do otherwise!

It was one of those dreadful rainy nights that lead to power cuts and landslides. The bus stop was dark and I could only see a figurine from a distance. The branding board at the back was dying, flickering once in a while. The sky greeted me with a gaze of lightning and thunder as I reached the bus stop. But the lightning and the timely flickering of the advertisement board gave me a good peek at the Goddess. I say Goddess because, for a moment, she reminded me of Aphrodite, the Greek Goddess of love. Auburn hair, light eyes, sharp nose, luscious lips, a supple body. She was wearing a blue dress which, in this setting, made her look divine. The sight stunned me for a few seconds and all I could utter was, “Need help?”. I could have extended that line with a lot of statements like, ‘I live close by’ or ‘I can drop you home’ or ‘I can stay with you'.

But the sheer beauty of the girl's face made me a retard. The girl asked if I could fetch a rickshaw for her. I did not say a word. I felt like a genie whose aim in life was to fulfill their master's wish. Somehow, I couldn't shrug off the girl's face from my mind. In any other situation or if I would have seen her face earlier, I wouldn't have had the courage to talk. But now I had. I had done it and there was no looking back. It was getting clearer now. God had His plan. Me leaving late from office, extreme rains, me having my bike that day, the girl getting stuck near my home. All of this could not be a coincidence. I was meant to meet this girl. Now, all I needed to do was catch a rickshaw for her. She'd thank me a ton and share her number. Then we'd soon catch up and take it forward. It was all set. Thank you, God. I kept looking for a rickshaw for the next half an hour. However, deep inside I was imagining my mother's reaction when I'd make them meet. She would have never imagined such a beautiful bride for me. Oh, I was so in love with her!

I finally got a rickshaw, asked the driver to follow me. When I approached the bus stop, I could see her talking to someone over her mobile. I knew I had to ask her number as soon as she'd disconnect. I allowed the rickshaw to overtake me and directed him towards the bus stop. The moment the rickshaw stopped at the bus stop, she took her bag and went and sat inside, while still talking on her mobile. I put the stand down to rest my bike and to go and talk to her. To my surprise, the rickshaw took off. I was sure that the girl would ask him to stop to talk to me or maybe, at least thank me. But no. The rickshaw zipped through the dark street with the sky pouring endlessly. I stood there in the rain for 2 minutes, alone and stunned. How could she be so thankless? How could she break my heart so ruthlessly? Or maybe, I was wrong. Any other night, she would have waited to talk to me but today…. today it rained.

If only one could tell true love from false love as one can tell mushrooms from toadstools.

- Katherine Mansfield

DANCE THE NIGHT AWAY

Today's typical urban lifestyle is an ample contradiction to the tried and tested methods of our past generations. We work hard and earn through the day to burn the same money to de-stress through the night. It's quite strange actually. Come to think of it, why do we earn at all if we can't even use it worthwhile? Or is it that we stress so that we can de-stress later? Well, all this sounds complicated, but my life wasn't so. My motto was very clear, work hard (as if I had an option), party harder.

Life at an advertising agency is very different from a corporate 9-5 job. Work-life balance doesn't exist here. But it came with a lot of extra perquisites. To start with, there is no dress code, and the atmosphere is very chill. People don't judge you for who you are. Also, stock their booze at the office. One odd day, you can even witness people smoking up in the so-called 'brainstorming' room. So, the moral of the story is that your atmosphere moulds you into a different being altogether. One, for whom the typical moralities of their parents don't generally hold. Now, me being a bachelor in a far-off city, away from my parents, was enjoying this phase of my life.

Four boys from four different states of India, staying together and making each day count. That is how my bachelor pad felt like. We had a simple rule, every Friday was meant for a disco night. A disco opened doors to all the necessary evils of our lives. Loud music, good food, ample booze, at times some spliffs, and most crucial, gorgeous women. As bachelors, the presence of women and the possibilities that followed motivated us. Being worked up through the week, we did not have the luxury of meeting new faces every day or going on fancy dates. So, the idea was to make the best use of the opportunity. We were always alert and on the hunt when we were out, partying.

"Oops, I am...... Raj. Hope you are fine." To be honest, I wanted to apologize to this girl for stomping her feet on the dance floor. But one look, and I couldn't miss the opportunity. She wasn't a typical 'beautiful' or 'hot' girl. Of course, she was hot but in a cute way. She was carrying a boy cut with golden streaks, had a petite frame, and was wearing the LBD with high-rise boots. She was killing the look, in short. Also, my actual name is Hemraj but at places like these, I prefer the name, Raj! Any guesses, why!!! Anyway, she said she was fine and got back to dancing with her friends. But now that we had spoken, I had to take it forward. So, I meticulously got into her circle of friends and continued dancing. Over time, it led to us talking to each other, the 'get to know each other' phase. The more we talked, the more she felt like my person. We had so much in common, our tastes were similar too. Obviously, I had to get her a refill. Duh!!! I generally considered these expenses as an investment but today, it felt different. It didn't feel like a burden. She even introduced me to her friends. It felt like we were meant to be. Something that had been missing in my life. We were perfect together. Rather than closing the night on a high, for the first time, I was looking to meet her again. I wanted to know more about her. Was I falling for her? I don't know for real, but this was definitely a new feeling, and I was so looking forward to figuring that out. At around 1:30 am, when the DJ announced the last track for the night, rather than making a move, I asked for her number. My intention was pious, and I wanted to catch up later. The thought of meeting her again gave me a tingling sensation. She obliged me with her number and pleased, we went our ways. For the first time in my life, I was less exhausted and more rejuvenated while leaving a disco.

The next day was Saturday and I woke up with a smile on my face. My agenda for the day was clear, call Pari and meet her. I dismissed all my roommates' plans in disdain and dialled her fabled number. "The number you have dialled is temporarily out of service." Oops... seemed the number needed a recharge. Well, I decided to wait till evening to see if she'd call. At around 5 pm, I was mentally drained. I hadn't heard from her yet. I tried her number again with the same result. In the heat of the moment, don't know what made me do this, I recharged the number. I was happy that nothing could stop our holy reunion now. This time when I called, the phone rang. Yet, the voice that answered didn't sound familiar. Turned out that the number belonged to someone staying in the outskirts of the city who had no clue about Pari. But he did thank me numerous times on knowing that it was me who had reactivated it for him. For him, not really, but his gratitude was the silver lining to this debacle.

The call ended. And so did my undying lust towards the female body. I was enlightened by the event, I felt lighter. Love wasn't skin deep. Maybe, the next Friday when I go to a disco, it would be to enjoy the moment, rather than to score. Maybe, I'll be free to just dance the night away.

It's sad to know I'm done. But looking back, I've got a lot of great memories.

- Bonnie Blair

IT WAS YOU

I was using public transport to head to school the other day. On the way, a middle-aged man came and sat next to me. Not that he smelt bad or pinched me but in an instant, I felt a strong repulsion from him. So much so that I left my seat after a while and went and stood near the door. What is it that made me so uncomfortable with him? One word, aura. The human energy field that either accepts or rejects another. But this wasn't my first encounter with the concept.

It was the last day of school before the summer vacation started. Almost everyone had plans to go out of town as next year would be difficult, considering it was the 10th board for us. However, my parents had enrolled me in a special career grooming program as I happened to be a bright chap. My father would often say, "These are the formidable years. A little hard work now will take you a long way in the future". To be honest, I didn't mind staying back because I loved my city and people way more than my relatives. Relatives, who stayed miles away in other cities of the country, I hardly knew. Yet, I was grieving more for the fact that Naveen, my best friend, was off to his cousin's place as well. Mobiles weren't prevalent then. So, two months without the usual banter and a special career program, five days a week, was going to be difficult. I wanted to meet and bid him adieu, one last time, after school. Hence, I kept looking for him. I ignored the fact that my transport had arrived, and any more delay could lead to me missing the bus. All of a sudden, I could feel a whiff of fragrance around me. I knew someone had brushed past me and the scent around me made me believe that it was a girl. I got this huge inclination to find out the identity of this person. It was like, I had to know. Remember the discussion about aura, this was my first encounter with the concept. It was like the perfect aura match. I tracked the smell like a hound and could see her back. A bunch of thick, curly hair, tied together in a knot, is all I could register. She was not from our school as she wasn't wearing our uniform. But, to make matters worse, she wasn’t wearing any other school’s uniform either.

Honk honk.... A minute more and I was on the verge of missing my transport. But...... but I had to see her face. That way, I could search for her later and maybe, get to know her. I had never felt this strong an urge to know a girl before. Neither was I a womanizer, nor a heavy extrovert. I was more of the studious kinds. Anyway, I had to rush to board the bus. Although, I made it a point to see her face while the bus crossed her. I was almost hanging out of the window but what I saw was well worth the effort. She had a beautiful round face with big, dreamy eyes and a perfect nose. Her full lips complemented the rest of the profile. She still carried a bit of baby fat on her body which was suiting her well. The highlight, however, was her curly tresses. I think she saw me too as she tucked a rebel ringlet to the back of her right ear with wide eyes and an open mouth. Guess, the visual was a little too dramatic. I didn't know what to do with this though. To begin with, the schools were shut for the next two months. Also, Naveen was unavailable as he was leaving the same night. But somehow, I couldn't get her face off my mind.

The next two months of holidays were pretty busy for me. I had newer concepts to learn at the program. On occasions, I enjoyed with my parents and sister over the weekends. Also, met a few new people who were scholars, like me. Other than me, there were a few others from my school too who were attending the program. I had enquired with everyone I knew if they had seen that girl on the last day. To some extent, for a surety that she was real and not a figment of my imagination. But also hoping that someone would know her in person and could direct me to her. All my efforts went in vain. It seemed everyone from my school had seen her, but no one knew her. Most of all, everyone had a viewpoint about her existence too. I had sailed way far into the ocean of naivety because I kept trying to check the suggested options. Finding her had become my holiday mission. She was like that passion that I couldn't pursue. The more I tried to forget her, the more she overpowered me. It was the strongest one-sided love someone would have heard of. The funny thing though was that I didn't know her identity. Nor was sure of the possibility of seeing her again in the future. But all this and more couldn't deter me from looking for her, thinking about her, and having imaginary conversations with her. In short, falling for her over and over again.

Finally, the day came when Naveen was returning home. The school was about to reopen the day later. I still hadn't found the girl with curls, nor had heard from anyone about her. Excited, I reached Naveen's house. I had so much to talk to him about. Naveen was the typical extrovert 'jack-of-all-trades' character who could orchestrate impossible solutions. His network was so strong that by her mere description, he could find her for me. It didn't matter, which school she belonged to. I was sitting in his living room waiting for him to turn up. But before him, came the same mesmerising smell I had been searching for the past two months. In came my fabled princess with a glass of juice. She put the glass on the table and asked, "Hey, aren't you the one who was jumping out of the bus's window?" I was way too stunned to react. She asked again, "Hello… you there?" I jolted back into the living world. "Ya. Hi… Ya, I was looking for someone. Who are you?", I asked. "Naveen's cousin. Who were you looking for?", she asked. "Guess, it was…. you", I said pointing at Naveen standing right behind her.

Searching is half the fun: life is much more manageable when thought of as a scavenger hunt as opposed to a surprise party.

- Jimmy Buffett

MAY GOD GRANT ALL YOUR WISHES

Death, one of the harshest realities of life. One can prepare oneself for it but can never shy away from it. Few deaths are traumatic for the deceased. Whereas almost all are painful for the close ones left behind. Grief is an extremely confusing emotion. No two people grieve the same way. Yet, come to think of it, death also opens multiple avenues. After all, life finds its way out and every mishap has a silver lining to it.

Mr. Pinto disconnected the call on his mobile and sank into the sofa of his living room. The living room of a 3 BHK apartment in a plush locality of Bandra. It was so silent that the drop of a pin could echo. But Mr. Pinto was exploding inside. He had just received the news of his best friend's passing away. They had been friends for over 45 years. All those times spent together sliding through his memory. He wanted to shout, cry, say so much but there was no one to listen to him. His apartment was not always this quiet. Not until his wife passed away a few years back. He also had a daughter and a son who were settled abroad. Now, Mr. Pinto was living a solitary life holding on to his wife's memories and his mobile phone, which enabled him to hear his children's voices.

Amidst all these years of loneliness, the only ray of hope for Mr. Pinto had been the evenings spent at Joseph's house. Joseph, his best friend, was no more. So, naturally, Mr. Pinto was heartbroken. Alone he sat and reminisced the good times spent together. A tiny drop of tear rolled down his left cheek. All of a sudden, his eyes widened, and his expression changed. Now that Joseph was gone, what about Maria? Maria was dead Joseph's wife. Their only daughter was married and settled abroad too. Should he allow Maria to live his life or should he intervene. Even if he intervened, what could he do? He couldn't propose Maria to come and stay with him. Or could he? What if they got married? Ever since the death of his wife, Mr. Pinto had always been jealous of Joseph. Maria was a beautiful lady who was aging with grace. Perhaps this would be the best solution to their common problem, Mr. Pinto thought to himself. Especially now that Joseph was gone. Of course, Joseph was gone. With that lingering thought, Mr. Pinto once again sank into the depths of grief. How could he think of such an obnoxious idea in such tormenting times, he ridiculed himself.

The next day, Mr. Pinto wore his best suit and went to attend Joseph's funeral. Maria, on seeing Mr. Pinto, broke down. She kept talking about their good old days together. She even told him that his presence made her feel closer to Joseph. Mr. Pinto remained calm and consoled her. Deep down, the thought of proposing Maria to get married still lingered in his mind. Today, he was not wearing his best suit to impress the soul of dead Joseph. It was meant for Maria. He was earnestly hoping that she would notice because there were times in the past when she had complimented him on this attire. But today was not his day.

The service progressed as the near and dear ones of the family kept coming in. Mr. Pinto was seated at one corner of the church. Even though he was surrounded by people, he was alone in his thoughts. He was still contemplating whether he should ask her out first and then pop the question. But could that make him sound like an opportunist? It was better if he kept the discussion serious and acted righteous. Maria should feel that he was proposing keeping her interest in mind. Amidst all this, Maria started her eulogy for Joseph. They had been together for 33 years. So that gave her a lot of memories to talk about. It was a trip down memory lane for Mr. Pinto too who was half-listening to her and half building up the mental strength to make his move. Suddenly, Maria's last statement caught all his attention and he turned pale. "With Joseph gone, I will be marrying Jesus now. I am sure, it will bring me closer to Joseph and he will be happy too", concluded Maria. She had decided to devote the remaining part of her life to the service of God. She was becoming a nun. People started walking up to congratulate her. Mr. Pinto got up from his chair too but with zero enthusiasm. He went up to Maria, touched her cheek with affection, looked at Joseph's picture, and said, "May the

Lord grant all your wishes." Once again, a tiny drop of tear rolled down his left cheek.

It's enough to indulge and to be selfish but true happiness is really when you start giving back.

- Adrian Grenier

THE CARELESS MAN

2020 was a strange year. No one was ready for what struck them. People didn't even know how to react. All that they could do was go with the flow. Do what was told to do by the authorities. Holding onto their near and dear ones, few became selfish. Also, few simply lost their way through. Largely, everyone became cautious and above all, avoided stepping out of their homes. I followed the same formula. April to June was a period of being homebound for me too. I stayed at a 1 BHK apartment in South Mumbai, on the 15th floor. Naturally, my take on my surroundings was reduced to a bird's eye view. Also, I was blinkered as I could not see 360 degrees from my apartment. Amidst all this mayhem and madness, one man often grabbed my attention.

South Mumbai skyscrapers have a lot of old, double and triple storeyed, buildings flanking them. In fact, it is the existence of these structures and the British architecture that add to the old town feel of it. My building had a few, along with a huddle of one-storey houses, to its left too. They did not fall in the way to my building nor were much visible. Still, me staying on the 15th floor had an ample view of the alley which led to the tiny, overpopulated houses. I often looked at the alley and imagined how difficult it would be for the residents to manage. Especially, during pandemic times. The alley was densely populated with people and low on sanitation too. These dwellings are often so congested that one patient could lead to a whole battalion of patients. Despite them being ticking time bombs and the authorities urging people to stay indoors, there lived an elderly man. One, I could repeatedly see getting out of his house and loitering on the empty streets. First of all, he was old. Second, it was not once or twice. He had to leave the safety of this house day in and day out, irrespective of the outbreak. The sheer carelessness and giving a toss to the society, infuriated me, every time I saw him leaving or returning to his home.

The said man had a tall, stylish personality. I am guessing, he would be 55 - 65 years old. But the reason that I could distinctively identify him every time, was his thick grey hair, middle-parted. It not just added to his looks but made him stand apart. Needless to say, suited him very well. Good looking or not, that did not give him the liberty to dishonour the safety of his surroundings. One day, I saw a cop approaching him while he walked towards the beginning of the alley, very slow. I was sure that he'd learn his lesson today. I was on the verge of celebrating when the cop wished him and passed by. What nonsense was that! The incident cemented a vague thought that had once crossed my mind. The man was a gangster. I was sure of it now. The man was not only anti-social, but the cops got intimidated by him too. What else could he be? Any human stepping out of their home was being beaten black and blue by the police. And this man, he was being wished. As if he was out for a very important job. I was sure that whatever reason he was out for, every day, was illegal.

I have never been a courageous woman or a rebel kind. But this man intrigued me to the hilt. One fine day, when I saw him leave his humble abode, I decided to follow him. I had heard of the power of social media. Today was the day to test the waters. I got double masked, wore my gloves, and carried a medical prescription, in case a cop stopped me. Cops who were party to this ghastly crime towards the society. I tiptoed behind him, the mobile camera switched on, peeking out of my jeans pocket. I was a girl on a mission. The old man sluggishly walked in front of me, carefree, wearing a simple, ordinary cloth mask. Disgraceful. But what I saw next shattered me from within. It is so easy to judge people from higher grounds, all righteous, full of moralities. The old man reached the end of the road and right outside the police station, sat next to a street bitch. She had a litter sucking on her tits. He gently patted the bitch on her head and brought out a packet of biscuits and a few slices of bread from his pocket and placed them next to her. Next, he got up carrying an empty bowl, filled it with water from the police station, and placed it next to the food. He sat there looking into the eyes of the new mother as she thanked him with all her heart. They weren't talking. Yet, there was so much being said. I was standing on the other side of the road watching this in awe. I was oblivious to the fact that my mobile camera was still recording this remarkable display of human emotion. A cop stopped by me and asked me to go home. He also said, “He is mad. This is his daily routine. Don’t risk your life, go home.” I nodded and started walking back towards my home with moist eyes. Towards my safe, urban home. The one full of moralities but no humanity. One thing that this incident proved to me was that humanity was not dead, even at the darkest hour of the century. Love was above all adversaries. And yes, the video went viral, and 'The Careless Man’ touched a million hearts.

Be ashamed to die until you have won some victory for humanity.

- Horace Mann

BEAUTY LIES IN THE EYES OF THE BEHOLDER

A plane versus a train. Which mode do you prefer to travel? Of course, with better connectivity and cheaper fares, planes have surpassed trains over time. A plane takes lesser time, provides better comfort, takes off, and lands at plush airports. Adds to the fun of travelling, isn't it? But how about the feeling of crossing over different states, getting to taste a variety of food items at the stations, knowing and spending time with strangers. Don't they add value to the general concept of travelling? It is true that our fast lives and a general lack of time don't allow frequent train travels for our generation. But it wasn't always this way. As a college student, living in a different state of the country, a train was my only mode of transport to get back home.

Train travels, especially during the peak seasons, had a lot of fun attached to them. The ideal time to book a ticket was three months before the date of travel. Duh!!! During college days, it was difficult to plan two days in a row, forget three months. So, at the most, three out of 10 in a group had tickets, and the rest piled on. That too, the three ticket holders used to be the ones whose tickets were couriered to them by their parents. Not that they were privileged. Their parents trusted them the least. For these, the chances of the booking money being spent on shopping were much higher. Hence, the tickets came from their parents so that there wasn't an iota of doubt left. Thankfully, for the rest, they were our confirmed berths. By berths, I meant sleeper class berths. AC tickets were too far-fetched to even think of. Yet, the beauty of sleeper class coaches was that they were 10 in number, all interconnected. Hence, even though not advisable, we had the freedom to loiter across the entire train. That gave us a better idea of which coach had the gorgeous women. On average, in every coach, there was at least one group that would be familiar with at least one of ours. Whichever coach had the better women, became our home for the next two days. Depending on the intervention of luck, the situation varied.

It was November and we were returning home for the Diwali vacation. Diwali was the worst time to travel because the trains were all pre-booked. Even the booking agents were incapable of getting the 'waiting list' tickets confirmed. We were 13 boys with 4 confirmed tickets. Of course, the number was unlucky, but fortune favours the brave. We had four berths, all in one cabin. The remaining berth owners frowned at us upon our arrival. They knew that their travel wasn't going to be pleasant, but no one dared to argue with college-goers. While others were busy accommodating their luggage, something far more interesting caught my eye.

Leaving a cabin after ours was seated a beautiful girl, on the single-seat side. Naturally, the one sitting at the corner of our lower berth had the chance of a direct eye contact. Before anyone could realise the situation, I sat at the corner and urged others to take the more comfortable seats. No one knew my real intention. The journey started and everyone settled down. I was uncomfortable but my visual gave me solace. The girl was dressed in an Indian salwar-kameez and had shades on. The sun rays touching her face, made it glow like gold. As the journey progressed, I noticed that she was accompanied by her family. They kept attending to her from time to time with food and other things. Other than talking to her family, by and large, she looked out of the window. Of course, she did notice me because I was staring at her, literally. She did not make a ruckus out of it though. I thought, maybe, she liked the attention. Maybe, she liked me. After a while, she put on her earphones and rested her head on the windowpane. Even through her sunglasses, I knew that her eyes were shut. That gave me the freedom to stare at her without any inhibition. Her face was not just beautiful, it had an uncanny calming effect. The more I saw it, the more peaceful I became. Perhaps, this journey was the means to reach my destination. Not my home but the destination of love. Her face intrigued me, and I was desperate to talk to her. I even brushed her shoulder once, on my way to the toilet. She was in a state of absolute tranquility. Train nights are usually early for all. Hence, the evening ended, and everyone settled for their disturbed sleep. We were awake as we did not have enough berths for 13 people to sleep. I hung on to my position and leaned on the side stand through the night. I was eager to see her morning face when she'd wake up, without the shades.

The next morning, I was late for the party. The people in the coach were already settled in, by the time I rose to senses. There she was, once again looking out of the window with her shades on. Well, I couldn't wear glasses for so long for sure. Nevertheless, I freshened up and decided to make the first move. I wrote my name and my email on a piece of paper and showed it to her, whenever she looked at me. But she ignored me completely. Probably, the presence of her family made her do so, I thought to myself. It was time to be a little braver and more discreet. I brushed past her and threw the chit, with my coordinates on it, at her like a ninja. Within seconds, I was sure that she was with me on this as there was no loud shouting behind me, as is the case otherwise. To my surprise, when I returned to my seat, I could see the chit untouched, lying by her legs. Did she not see that coming or was she just acting pricey! Over the next few hours, I gestured towards the chit several times, which was difficult as I was surrounded by people. Unfortunately, all my efforts went in vain. Finally, a man from her family came up to her. While speaking with her, picked up the chit, opened it, saw here and there, and threw it outside. She was laughing and talking to him as if clueless about the incident. I was looking elsewhere during this event. So, the man didn't doubt my intention. But the situation certainly intrigued me more. I had to unravel the truth. Why was she behaving so cold after giving positive signals? She knew I had been looking at her throughout and she had approved it. The journey was coming to an end, and I had to get closure.

While crossing her to alight at the station, I deliberately dropped a small bag on her lap. To my utter surprise, she got shocked and panicked, as if she couldn't see it. I apologised and tried to calm her. The man who had thrown the chit out approached her and appeased her. Also, he addressed me by my name and said, "Don't be surprised. She is blind. You please carry on." The words not only gave me a closure but also brought an abrupt end to my fairy-tale. I stood at the station looking at her sitting by the window. As the train whistled, I lifted my arm to wave at her one last time. The man, sitting next to her, looked at me puzzled. As if, questioning my comprehension capabilities. I had heard him clear and knew that she couldn't see me. But it was too hard for me to let go. I wanted to remember her in my own way. Though not real, it was beautiful. After all, beauty lies in the eyes of the beholder.

Sometimes it's the journey that teaches you a lot about your destination.

- Drake

DO NOT CROSS THE LINE

What is Love? Love is an emotion that leads to certain chemical imbalances in the body that lead to the secretion of certain hormones. Nowhere in this equation does procreation fall into place. Then why do we keep associating love with gender? Why is it so difficult to accept two people of the same gender, falling in love? Forget about the past. Even now, after laws getting lenient towards the issue, individuals feel hesitant to open up about their preferences. Such is the societal pressure surrounding this topic. There is a general sense of homophobia lurking amongst us which is somehow considered normal. Normalcy for the majority becomes a dreaded silence for a few.

I am a 32-year-old gay who has fought 30 years of his life to come out of the closet. Of course, the initial years didn't matter. When it started to matter, I had nowhere to go. Hailing from a tier 3 city, as a teen, I considered myself to be ailing. I had to fake ogle at girls to be a part of the circle I belonged to or tried to belong to. Whereas, in reality, it was their brothers whom I found attractive. I couldn't even think of discussing it with my parents. Forget sexual preference, even sex as a topic was taboo. Only after moving to a bigger city for higher education did I realise that there was nothing wrong with me. It was natural and what was ailing was societal thinking. Still, I didn't dare to come out to my parents. It was a couple of years back, when I was 20,000 feet under the pressure to get married, that I confronted my mother. Her initial expression was something to look out for. Then she concluded that it was all her mistake. Supposedly, she should have encouraged me to mingle more with girls. Finally, it was my friends' mistake who had misled me in life. I sat and heard her out. To be honest, the situation was hilarious but all I could do was carry a straight face and empathise with her. I am sure that my mother would have discussed it with my father. Yet, we never spoke about it. Over time, my parents stopped expecting me to get married.

Staying in a metro city, away from my parents, definitely helped me to flourish. I worked at a multinational firm and was living my life on my terms. Gay or straight, no one questioned me here. Still, as they say, your upbringing lingers with you. Only my close-knit circle knew about my sexuality. For the rest, I was a normal guy. No one was asking, nor was I upfront disclosing. Life was at peace. I was doing well at work until one day when I was introduced to Diljeet. Diljeet was a young guy with a similar kind of experience as mine. He had recently joined the organization and we were supposed to work together on a project. As gays, it is often said that we have a "gay radar" that lets us know when we are around other gays. It is nothing but a vibe that straight men do not understand. I knew that my radar couldn't mistake but Diljeet came through as a pretty 'normal', women ogling guy. At first, I thought that he was bi, one who swung both ways. Then felt, he still didn't know. Later, after spending a lot of time together, realised that he very well knew but did not dare to get out. Trust me, it is difficult and is a personal choice. But I didn't like his reason. The very reason I chose to come out was that I didn't want to ruin a girl's life. Diljeet, on the other hand, was all-in for his parents. He was ready to sacrifice a girl's life for the dignity of his parents, plus live with an everyday compromise. As I said, it's a personal choice but I did try to talk about the pros and cons of both situations with him. We differed on some points, but these conversations brought me closer to him. Diljeet was a good-looking bloke, 29, a cut surd. The more time we spent together, which was obvious because we worked together, I grew fonder of him. It was fun working with him, the evening hangouts were great too. Plus, there was a strong sexual tension between us which was quite interesting. I did offer him a few times, but he rejected me. He believed that he was at the threshold and if he crossed the line, he would not be able to hold back. Made sense for him but the rejections never offended me. I had gone through this door once and believed that sooner or later, he would too. Then, I would be the one welcoming him with open arms. I was ready to be patient with Diljeet.

Monday morning, I was looking for Diljeet at work. Figured that he had taken a leave. Well, forgot to mention to me, I thought to myself. I tried calling him, but he didn't answer. So, I carried on with my day. The next day, he informed that his parents had visited over the weekend.

Also, he would be going home for a few weeks, a month later. I got suspicious but he appeased me with a reason. Apparently, there was some function at his place where his presence was necessary. Sounded right to me. We moved on. The next few weeks, we worked hard on the project, also our evenings became more entertaining. On the evening of his last day, before he was off for his leave, he handed me an invitation card. By now, we were seemingly drunk. I was confused for a few seconds. When I inquired as to what was it, he said, "Please do come." Then he turned, looked back at me, and left without saying another word. I was still bemused. In a drunken stupor, I opened the envelope and took the card out. It wrote, "Diljeet Singh weds Simran Kaur". He had decided not to cross the line, ever.

Love is the answer, and you know that for sure; Love is a flower, you've got to let it grow.

- John Lennon

LIFE IMPRISONMENT SENTENCE

The first time I saw her here, I knew that she would not be able to survive. Prison isn't made for soft people. Of course, I have seen people changing. But clearly, she lacked intent. Time indeed changes people. But more than that, it is the time spent here that messes one up. For a few, the change makes them peaceful. I feel they are the ones who use the isolation well and embrace their inner self. Guess, that is what a sentence is meant for. Yet, most do not get there. Either their thoughts or the prison walls, they get engulfed over time. Also, time works very differently here. So, it is up to an individual to make the best out of it.

I am no expert on the topic but 13 years in the service does give you an insight. Yes, I am not an inmate here. Rather, I am on the other side of the table. A women's prison is very different from its counterparts. Not physically, but spiritually. Crime is more of a man's world and statistics prove it. Women continue to be a minority in all parts of the world, the percentage being less than 10. Moreover, when they manage to come here, they come with a lot of baggage. Also, their mindset is very different compared to the male inmates. Over time, I have seen women from different age groups, social classes, and circumstances come here. Everyone reacts in their own way. Few of them howl, silently cry, a few get angry, some lose their mental balance, and some go quiet. As if, acceptance just dawned upon them, and their wait was over. That was the case with Seema. No tears, no repentance, yet cocooned inside. Since the day she came here, she had not spoken a single word with anyone. She woke up, ate, slept. As if, she had sentenced herself to solitary confinement. She had been brought in for the murder of her entire family comprising of a husband, two kids, and her own set of parents. People said that she was mad. Supposedly, she did so under the influence of a Godman. Her family, now dead, was meant to resurrect post the sacrifice. Well, that does sound like the work of somebody mentally unstable. Due to all these reasons, she did not get a death sentence. Instead, she was left here to rot for the rest of her life.

Seema Jain was a well-to-do doctor, in fact, a child specialist. Theirs was an educated family, her husband was a doctor too. Could a fraud Godman infuse so much faith in them? Of course, he could and hence she was here. But what could have been the other reasons that led her to this? No one knew what she thought about the event later. The law took its course and sentenced her within its boundaries. But did it do justice to the event? Maybe, the family wanted her to do this. In that case, who did the justice go to? The lady was merely doing what everyone wanted her to. She was nothing but the ashes of a burnt tree. All these questions intrigued me, and I started looking for opportunities to meet Seema.

I am Manju Kokre, a 38 year old constable in the force. I got this job when my husband lost his life fighting with the terrorists in the 26/11 Mumbai attack. I had no one left to look up to in my life. The jail, to most people, was a dreaded place to be. But for me, I found peace here. A purpose that was thoroughly missing in my life otherwise. I did double shifts most of the days. Spending time with the inmates gave me a reason to exist. I so wanted to help Seema but somehow, she didn't open doors for anyone. Such docile women get badly bullied in the prison and so was the case with her. Still, I protected her whenever I could. Over time, the word spread that I had a soft corner for Seema, so no one was to disturb her. Soft corner, huh!! Maybe it was less of that and more of a reflection of me that I saw in her. I had been there 13 years back and I survived. I wanted her to survive too. We developed a silent language between the two of us. I loved to go and meet her and think, she liked me visiting too. Sometimes, we would just sit outside her cell and watch into thin air for hours. Words did not matter anymore. We gave each other a sense of belongingness, something that was missing in both our lives. I even got home-cooked food for her at times. She ate in silence but never cared to tell me whether she liked it or not. Considering the food available at the jail, I was sure she did. At times, when I met her after a gap, I could see that glee in her eyes. Without a word spoken, we had found companionship in each other's presence. I liked doing things for her.

Although all inmates were like family members to me, she was special. Her silence brought the best out of me. Perhaps, I was waiting for the day she'd talk to me.

One rainy night, at around 3:30 am, I got a call to report urgently at the prison. I had returned home from my shift at 10:00 pm. Anyway, I freshened up and left in haste, imagining what would have happened in 5 hours. When I reached, I was asked to head straight to Seema's cell. Panicked, I reached to find Seema soaked in blood. I shouted for help but guess, it was too late for that. She had found something sharp and slit her wrist, God knows when. By then she had lost too much blood and was practically pale. She tapped on my wrist with her fragile fingers, her head on my lap. When I looked at her, she finally said her first words to me, "Thank you and sorry" and then her soul left her body. I sat there with her lifeless body thinking how brave she was. She dared to end it all. Whereas I chose to live through my life imprisonment sentence.

You do the right thing even if it makes you feel bad. The purpose of life is not to be happy but to be worthy of happiness.

- Tracy Kidder

MOM REMEMBERS EVERYTHING

"Hello... Prateek? Gogol this side. Could you please visit my house for some time this evening? Nothing to worry but it's a little urgent." That was Mr......... sorry, Dr. Gogol Dasgupta, a Fellow of Royal College of Surgeons (FRCS). A renowned neurosurgeon. One, who had travelled across the globe, witnessed different cultures of the world, and worked with an innumerable number of patients. Now settled in his big, cozy apartment in South Kolkata. Unlike neighbouring apartments, his house had no state-of-the-art gadgets, no fancy drapery, and not too many people either. A glance across the apartment and all one could see was an old school Bengali charm, two huge dogs, and Dr. Dasgupta, reading on his century-old rocking chair. Even after years of research on the human mind and treating numerous patients with today's modern-day medicines, he still believed that aesthetics and acoustics played a huge role in shaping up the human brain. Or was he lying to himself and clearly hoping for a miracle?

Dr. Dasgupta, now 61 years old, had worked hard for what he had achieved. He got an ample number of opportunities to settle abroad. In fact, he was offered a green card to settle in the USA as well. But he was sure to return to India. Not that he was a patriot at heart; he strongly believed that Indian health infrastructure was way behind developed countries. He had to take care of his mother, back in India. Gogol lost his father when he was 15. Extremely talented that he was from a young age, a teen without a father lacks the motivation to grow. It was then that his mother stepped up and pushed him to perform. It was her sheer dedication and single-focused attention towards Gogol that led him to his scholarship and subsequently his dreams. No one could ever imagine the condition that this powerful lady was in, today.

The human brain is complex. Even after years of research and development, modern medical science is yet to unravel the mysteries within. Of course, medication and modern facilities provide relief or delay the inevitable but cannot deter nature to take its course. Comparing a human being to a machine, how would it be if the human brain could be refreshed with the click of a button? Sounds insane or annihilistic but that is exactly what Alzheimer's does, over a period of time. Dr. Dasgupta, being a neurosurgeon himself, was mentally prepared for the time when his mother wouldn't recognise him. It was almost five years now that his mother had stopped recognising anyone. All she remembered was her childhood and glimpses from the past. Preparing for these days, Gogol never thought of marrying and starting a family of his own. In the initial years, he did not have the time to plan. By the time he settled and could plan, his mother had developed a mild cognitive impairment. Being an expert himself, he knew how this would end. Also, to add to his misery, his mother could not recognise him but remembered that she had a son who was a doctor. Gogol would sit for hours and listen to his mother blabbering and complaining. She would talk about how her son would come from foreign lands and take her away with him. She even threatened Gogol with complaining to her son if he didn't get her what she had asked for. Dr. Dasgupta did try often to talk to her as himself, but she did not budge. He often imagined what would it be like if she ever recognised him or accepted him as her son. What would the conversation be like?

Prateek was greeted with a big hug by Dr. Dasgupta at his South Kolkata home. The house was well lit and beaming with energy. That evening was going to be different. Gogol's long-term dream of spending a few hours with his mother had peaked and he couldn't resist it anymore. "Prateek, I want you to meet my mother for a few hours, being me", said Dr. Dasgupta. Prateek was taken aback. The poor soul looked at Dr. Dasgupta, puzzled. He explained to him further that his mother remembered that she had a son and had instructed him to call for him. The observations would help him in further treatment. Prateek, a little shaken, agreed to his trusted friend. A few minutes later, Dr. Dasgupta entered her room and announced in glee, "Maa, see Gogol's here to meet you." The 83-year-old woman turned and got up from the bed. Her eyes shone. She was meeting her son after, roughly, 15 odd years.

The human mind can play vicious games and so was one blooming in Gogol's mind. If only he could seize this moment forever. The next few hours, the old lady talked non-stop to Prateek, the face, and Gogol, the talker. She spoke about a lot of things, right from Gogol's school days to how great it would be when he gets married. She even mentioned his father for a moment and sniffled a little. Occasionally, she would ask something and Prateek either nodded or looked at Dr. Dasgupta with hesitance. Few stories even scandalized him. For instance, when Dr. Dasgupta's mother spoke of the first time when Gogol shat in his pants, at school. Or when she caught his first love letter. The conversation had opened a pandora's box which was tightly shut for many years. Gogol was thoroughly enjoying it and was reliving his entire life in a few hours. He had no shame but tons of satisfaction on his face. It was the most heartfelt conversation that both had had in a long time. Practically, both were in tears, but these were happy tears. Finally, both had attained peace.

The event had exhausted Gogol's mother and soon, she dozed off. Dr. Dasgupta and Prateek did not talk for a while as both were engrossed in their thoughts. Finally, at the door, Prateek couldn't resist saying, "Ummm… Dr. Dasgupta, Alzheimer's or no Alzheimer's, after what I witnessed today, I am 100 percent convinced that Mom remembers everything!" Both had a hearty laugh at this. Gogol was relieved and Dr. Dasgupta, he was the drowning man who had just caught on a straw.

Happiness, true happiness, is an inner quality. It is a state of mind. If your mind is at peace, but you have nothing else, you can be happy. If you have everything the world can give – pleasure, possessions, power – but lack peace of mind, you can never be happy.

- Dada Vaswani

Notes

Dedicated to the greatest teacher of all, Life. Also, Lord Shiva and Goddess Kali, the beginning and end of all.

Didibhai and Meshomoni, if you were around, I am sure that this would have been your prized possession. Hoping to make you proud, wherever you are.

www.ingramcontent.com/pod-product-compliance
Lightning Source LLC
LaVergne TN
LVHW050425160726
843469LV00041B/1230